Chapter One

London, 1870

IT PREYS ON THOSE WHO WALK ALONE THROUGH THE PARK AT NIGHT.

WHAT DOES?
THE DEMON, *SPRING HEELED JACK.*
IT'S SAID TO HAVE THE EYES OF THE DEVIL AND THE BREATH OF HELL FIRE.

AND IT CAN JUMP HIGHER THAN THE TALLEST TREE... HOGWASH.
BESIDES, REPORTS INDICATE SPRING HEELED JACK ONLY HAS AN INTEREST IN *WOMEN.*

THEN YOU WILL UNDERSTAND MY INSISTENCE THAT A BRAVE LAD SUCH AS YOURSELF ESCORT ME.

DO YOU BELIEVE IN *SPIRITS?*
OF COURSE NOT.
NEITHER DID EBENEZER SCROOGE, UNTIL THREE GHOSTS PAID HIM A VISIT.

MIGHT WE TALK ABOUT ANOTHER CHARLES DICKENS STORY?

HOOT
OLIVER TWIST, PERHAPS?

DON'T BE SO QUICK TO WRITE OFF THE *DEAD.*

CLICK

SCREEEEECH

GET DOWN!

FWWATT

KRAK

WHUMP

YOU'RE CHARLES DICKENS.
ASTUTE OBSERVATION.

SPRING-LOADED STILTS. HE'S A THIRD RATE CIRCUS PERFORMER AT BEST.
NEXT TIME WILL BE DIFFERENT.
YOU SAID THAT THE LAST TIME, AND THE TIME BEFORE THAT.
IF PROVING THE PARANORMAL WERE EASY, WHAT PURPOSE WOULD WE SERVE?

AND WHO IS THIS?
ARTHUR-- ARTHUR CONAN DOYLE, SIR.
REMEMBER, YOUNG DOYLE, WHAT YOU WANT TO BELIEVE HAS NO BEARING ON THE TRUTH.
MANY TRUTHS LIE HIDDEN. THE AFTERLIFE IS ONE OF THEM.

WE NEED MORE.

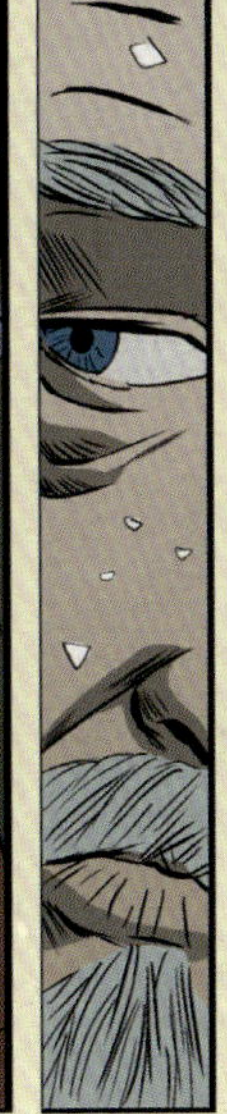

GO WALLACE, BUT SOMEDAY I'LL PROVE TO YOU I'M RIGHT.

YOU'LL COME TO LEARN THAT NOT ALL EVIDENCE IS MATERIAL.
SOME THINGS CAN ONLY BE EXPERIENCED.

The InSpectres

30 Years Later

for Sherlock
mystery was

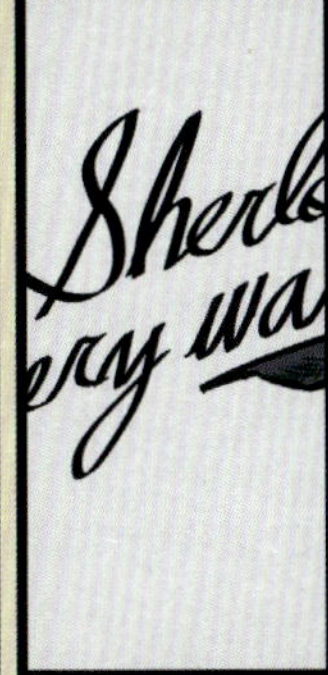
Sherl
ery wa

TRY NOT TO OVEREXERT YOURSELF, MRS. DOYLE.

THUMP

THE NEW ARABIAN NIGHTS
ROBERT LOUIS STEVENSON

YOU CAN STOP PRETENDING TO WORK, ARTHUR. THE DOCTOR HAS GONE.

NONSENSE. I'VE BEEN SLAVING AWAY.

LET'S SEE WHAT YOU'VE WRITTEN, THEN.

HMM, I AGREE, THIS IS DREADFUL.
WHY DO I NEED TO BRING HIM BACK FROM THE DEAD?

THE PEOPLE MISS SHERLOCK HOLMES, DEAR.

HE'S DEAD FOR A REASON.
WE DEMAND HIS TRIUMPHANT RETURN.

THINGS END.
IT'S A FACT WE ALL MUST ACCEPT.

HAVE YOU ACCEPTED IT?

I THINK YOU NEED A BREAK. COME ALONG, GET DRESSED.
FOR WHAT?

TO PAINT THE TOWN RED.

NOT THIS YEAR. TRISTAN'S INSUFFERABLE.

WE CAN DANCE.
DOCTOR SAID NOT TO EXERT YOURSELF.
YOU WERE EAVESDROPPING.
HIS VOICE CARRIES-- AND YOU NEED PROPER BED REST.

ON SECOND THOUGHT, IT WON'T BE FUN. YOU'LL SUCK THE JOY OUT OF IT.
I'M GLAD WE AGREE.
TOO BAD YOU'LL BE GOING ALONE, THEN.

THE INVITATION DID NOT COME FROM TRISTAN.
THIS MAGICIAN IS ALL THE RAGE IN AMERICA--
--AND APPARENTLY A BIG FAN OF YOURS.

MAGIC'S NOT REAL. PARLOR TRICKS.
MUST YOU EXAMINE EVERYTHING? ENJOY YOURSELF.
OR IF YOU PREFER WE CAN CHAT FOR HOURS ABOUT LIFE...

PERHAPS A BREAK IS A GOOD IDEA.

HE'S NOT DEAD, IS HE?

WHO?

SHERLOCK HOLMES, OF COURSE.

ANOTHER *CRAZED* FAN.

I'M *AGATHA.* AND YES, I LOVE YOUR BOOKS, BUT I'M NOT CRAZED.
CLEARLY. HOW DID YOU KNOW I WOULD BE HERE?
MY MOTHER HAS THE GIFT OF *SECOND SIGHT.* SHE INSISTED YOU WOULD ARRIVE ON THE ONE O'CLOCK.
IT'S *EIGHT.*
YOU'RE HERE, AREN'T YOU?

SHE ALSO READS *FORTUNES* AND TALKS TO THE *DEAD.*
I'VE ATTEMPTED TO PROVE MYSELF IN THE FAMILY TRADE--

--BUT I'M QUITE INEPT.
SHE SAYS I'M LESS TROUBLE BURIED IN A GOOD BOOK.

JUST TELL ME, WILL THERE BE ANOTHER *ADVENTURE?*

SOON.
OH, EXCELLENT! YOU CAN GIVE ME THE PLOT DETAILS NEXT TIME.

NEXT TIME?

The AMERICAN SENSATION HARRY "HANDCUFF" HOUDINI
HOUDINI has Broken
Chains, Prison Cell:

Tenth Annual
Paint The Town Red
THESE LOCKS WOULD SUBDUE LONDON'S MOST NOTORIOUS CRIMINALS--

--BUT I'M HARRY HOUDINI.

YOU CAN PUT AWAY YOUR KEY, INSPECTOR ATWOOD.

殭屍

MR. DOYLE, I PRESUME?

MORE APPROPRIATELY DRESSED, I SEE.
I PREFER THE COMFORT OF CHAINS TO THIS CONTRAPTION.
THIS IS MY WIFE, BESS.
I HEAR *SHERLOCK'S* COMING BACK.

YES, HE SENT ME A LETTER ANNOUNCING HIS RETURN.

SHOULD BE AT THE TRAIN STATION IN TWENTY MINUTES.
I SEE... IF YOU'LL PARDON ME, I MUST USE THE LOO, AS YOU BRITS LIKE TO CALL IT.

I'M SCOTTISH; WE CALL IT THE *LIBRARY.*

UM... YES, THE LIBRARY. RIGHT.

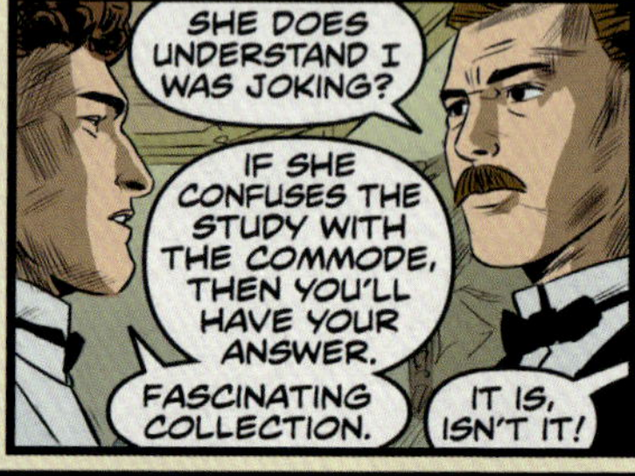

SHE DOES UNDERSTAND I WAS JOKING?
IF SHE CONFUSES THE STUDY WITH THE COMMODE, THEN YOU'LL HAVE YOUR ANSWER.
FASCINATING COLLECTION.
IT IS, ISN'T IT!

HELLO, *TRISTAN.*
THAT HANDSOME DEVIL IS MY GREAT GRANDFATHER, *MARQUESS GEORGE HEMSFORD.* THIS WAS HIS HOME; THESE WERE HIS THINGS.
THE TIME HAS COME ONCE AGAIN!
THE *STORY?*

"PRECISELY! THE STORY."
AS WITH TRADITION, MY FAMILY HAS DEMANDED I CEASE THESE FESTIVITIES.

AND IN KEEPING WITH THE TRADITION, MY ANSWER IS--

NO!

WHAT'S THE POINT OF THIS?
THIS STORY IS AN EMBARRASSMENT TO THE HEMSFORD FAMILY NAME.
FOR YEARS THEY'VE TRIED TO HIDE THIS HISTORY, BUT TRISTAN EMBRACES IT.
WARTS AND ALL.

I HAVE A TALE OF A MAN OBSESSED WITH THE SUPERNATURAL.
SO MUCH SO, HIS FAMILY DISOWNED HIM AND THE WORLD THOUGHT HIM MAD.

HE TRAVELED FAR AND WIDE TO FIND THE KEYS TO *EVERLASTING* LIFE, BUT HIS SEARCH PROVED FRUITLESS.
VILIFIED AND RIDICULED, HE DESPERATELY WANTED TO SHOW HIS CRITICS THAT THE REALM BEYOND THE LIVING WAS AS REAL AS THE PAINT ON THEIR DOORSTEP.

MY GREAT GRANDFATHER DECIDED HE WOULD WEAR THE FACE OF THE OTHER-WORLDLY...

... AND ALONG WITH HIS COHORTS, *PAINTED* LONDON FAR AND WIDE THE BRIGHT HUE OF *RED*.

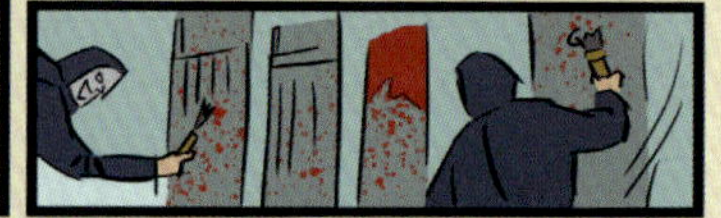

IN THIS ONE ACT, THE LEGEND OF SPRING HEELED JACK WAS BORN!
LABELED A PUBLIC NUISANCE, MY GREAT GRAND-FATHER WAS SUMMARILY *OSTRACIZED* FROM SOCIETY.
ON HIS DEATH BED HE SWORE *THAT, SOMEDAY,* HE WOULD PROVE ONCE AND FOR ALL THAT SPIRITS WALK AMONG US.

BOOM

LADIES AND GENTLEMEN, LISTEN TO ME!

YOU HAVE GATHERED TONIGHT TO HEAR TALL TALES--
--AND APPLAUD TRICKSTERS!

IS THIS PART OF THE SHOW?
NO.

YOU ARE NOT WELCOME, LOMAX.

YOU'RE A JEALOUS BLOW-HARD, UPSET THAT I HIRED A MORE FAMOUS MAGICIAN.

ANY MAN CAN ESCAPE A LOCK.
I, LOMAX LUMINARY, HAVE THE POWER TO ESCAPE DEATH!

SOON, YOU WILL BE PART OF THE REAL SHOW. ONE THAT WILL CHANGE... YOUR... AFTER-LIFE!

WHERE DID HE GO?

TIME FOR US TO DISAPPEAR?
I KNOW THE PERFECT PLACE.

WHICH CARD WAS IN YOUR MIND?
ACE OF SPADES.

I SUSPECT THE ACE OF SPADES WAS PREDETERMINED. THE TRUE ILLUSION WAS MAKING ME BELIEVE I HAD A CHOICE.

YOU HAVE THE MIND OF A MAGICIAN.

HAVE YOU EVER HEARD OF LOMAX LUMINARY?
NO, BUT HE MAY HAVE FIGURED OUT THE PERFECT DISAPPEARING ACT. ONE I'M DETERMINED TO DISCOVER--
--OR PERHAPS HE SPEAKS THE TRUTH, AND HAS A CONNECTION TO THE DEAD.
I ASSURE YOU, THE EXPLANATION IS MORE GROUNDED IN REALITY.

UNLESS YOU HAVE SEEN THE AFTERLIFE, YOU CAN'T MAKE THAT ASSURANCE.

HOW DO YOU DO THAT WITH YOUR EYES?
DO WHAT?

THUMP

THE STRANGE CASE OF DR. JEKYLL AND MR. HYDE.
ODD, THAT'S THE SECOND STEVENSON BOOK TO FALL TONIGHT.

HE WROTE THIS TO YOU?
To my dearest friend whom I have yet to meet R.L.

WE CORRESPONDED. ROBERT LIVED IN SAMOA. POOR SOUL, NEVER A DAY OF HEALTH.
HIS ENTIRE LIFE WAS CONSUMED BY ILLNESS. WE HOPED TO MEET, BUT HE PASSED ON BEFORE THE OPPORTUNITY PRESENTED ITSELF.

ARE YOU TRYING TO KILL ME?
ONLY ENOUGH TO SEE THE DEAD.
WHAT DO WE TOAST TO?
TO OUR WIVES.
WOULD YOU LIKE TO MEET HIM TONIGHT?
ABSINTHE FROM HUNGARIA.
SOME SAY IN THE WITCHING HOUR GHOSTS MIGHT BE SEEN WITH ITS AID.
BESS?
I LEFT HER AT THE PARTY!
GOODNIGHT, DOYLE.

KOFF
KOFF

SLIDE
THWAP
DICKENS?

YOU REMEMBER ME? GOOD. I HAVE LITTLE *TIME*.
WHERE IS IT?
WHERE'S WHAT?
TELL ME YOU STILL HAVE *IT*.

FOLLOW THE *EVIDENCE*, ARTHUR.

FIND *STEVENSON*.

IF YOU'RE REFERRING TO ROBERT LOUIS STEVENSON, HE'S *DEAD*--

--AND YOU'RE *NOT* REAL.
ONLY THE *INSPECTRES*, ARTHUR!
A CHRISTMAS CAROL

EVIDENCE IS NOT ALWAYS *MATERIAL*.
SPRING HEELED JACK *APPROACHES*... *BLOOD* WILL RUN... MANY WILL *DIE*.

FIND STEVENSON!

BONK

Westminster Abbey

SAINT MICHAEL THE ARCHANGEL, DEFEND US IN BATTLE. BE OUR *PROTECTION* AGAINST--

WILLIAM SHAKESPEARE
BURIED AT STRATFORD-ON-

Chapter Two

WHAT ON EARTH ARE YOU WEARING?
I TOLD YOU, I HAVE A DRIVING LESSON TODAY.

YOU CAN'T FAULT ME FOR WANTING AN ESCAPE FROM THE RACKET YOU PUT ON LAST NIGHT.
WHAT WAS IT YOU HEARD?

SOMEONE SHOUTING... "WHERE IS IT, WHERE IS IT?"... AND ALL THAT THRASHING ABOUT.
IT WAS LOUD ENOUGH TO WAKE THE DEAD.

PERHAPS YOU SHOULD JOIN ME. A JAUNT THROUGH THE COUNTRYSIDE COULD DO YOU SOME GOOD.
I HAVE OTHER MATTERS TO ATTEND TO.

DRIVING LESSONS... SHOULDN'T YOU BE RESTING?
SHOULDN'T YOU BE WRITING?
HAVE A WONDERFUL DRIVE, DARLING.

SPATENBEER
HAVE YOU HEARD?
MURDER AT THE ABBEY!
BLOOD EVERYWHERE!
SPRING HEELED JACK?
DON'T FILL YOUR HEAD WITH SUCH THINGS.

ARTHUR CONAN DOYLE COULD SOLVE IT. HE'S THE GREATEST DETECTIVE IN THE WORLD.
HE'S A WRITER.
STORIES MUST BE SOLVED TOO.

HE'S MY FRIEND, YOU KNOW.
SURE HE IS, KID.

LATEST SPECIAL

MURDER

PRIEST FOUND DEAD

MYSTERY SWIRLS AS LEGEND OF SPRING HEELED JACK RETURNS

DO YOU TAKE ME FOR A *FOOL?*
OF COURSE NOT.
INSTEAD YOU WOULD HAVE ME BELIEVE A WEALTHY ENGLISHMAN JUST *GRABS* A MAN AND FORCES HIM--

HELLO, MRS. HOUDINI. IT'S WONDERFUL TO SEE YOU AGAIN.
I'M GOING TO *STEAL* YOUR HUSBAND.

C'MON... LET'S GO.
YOU *SEE?*

Westminster Abbey
DICKENS VISITS YOU--
IT WASN'T DICKENS.
YOU SAID YOUR WIFE HEARD HIM.
SHE HEARD ME-- AIDED BY YOUR DRINK.

I SEE, SO YOU WARN YOURSELF THAT SPRING HEELED JACK IS ABOUT TO ATTACK. AND YOU SAID--
BLOOD WILL RUN.
WELL, THERE'S PLENTY OF THAT, ISN'T THERE?
DID YOU HAVE ANY PHYSICAL CONTACT WITH YOUR-- HALLUCINATION?

A BOOK MIGHT HAVE FALLEN ON MY HEAD.
MAYBE IT WAS A SIGN.
I DON'T BELIEVE IN SIGNS.

IF YOU SAY SO.
CHARLES DICKENS
BORN 7TH FEBRUARY 1812
DIED 9TH JUNE 1870

THIS ABBEY HAS BEEN SEALED--

DETECTIVE ATWOOD, WE WERE JUST PASSING BY, AND COULDN'T HELP TO--
INVOLVE YOURSELF IN POLICE MATTERS--I UNDERSTAND.

"I'M SURE SCOTLAND YARD CAN HANDLE IT FROM HERE."

HAVE YOU HEARD THE RUMORS THIS WAS SPRING HEELED JACK?
YES, BUT HIS ALIBI CHECKS OUT. WE'RE SHIFTING OUR FOCUS TO THE INVISIBLE MAN--
--I HOPE WE CAN FIND HIM.

IN ALL SERIOUSNESS, INSPECTOR, I'M AWARE I'M NOT A DETECTIVE, BUT--
NO, YOU'RE NOT. INCIDENTALLY, I DON'T LIKE SHERLOCK HOLMES... HE'S A KNOW-IT-ALL.
AS FOR MAGIC, WELL, A PROFESSION BASED ON LIES ISN'T MUCH OF A PROFESSION NOW IS IT?

I WAS TOLD THE BRITISH ARE POLITE.
AS THEY HURL INSULTS, YES.

SOMETHING STIRS.

ITS EYES WERE AFLAME. CLOTHES SOAKED IN BLOOD. IT STALKED PAST ME AS I HID, FEARING FOR MY LIFE.
WAS IT SPRING HEELED JACK?

IT COULD BE NONE OTHER.

"THE WRETCHED CREATURE JUMPED INTO THE AIR--"
"--AND SAILED ABOVE THAT WALL, YONDER."

IF I'M HEARING CORRECTLY, THIS PERSON LEAPT OVER THAT WALL?
PERSON? NO. A DEMON!

THAT THING WITH YOUR EYES. ARE YOU DOING THAT FOR GHOULISH EFFECT?
DOING WHAT?

T.H.
LONDON
ELECTRICAL
CORPORATION

THE FOREMAN HAS NOTHING TO REPORT.

ANY THOUGHTS?
IF THERE IS ANY CREDENCE TO WHAT THAT BYSTANDER SAID--

AND THE CULPRIT LEPT OVER THE WALL--

--HE WOULD HAVE LANDED HERE, LEAVING A FOOT *IMPRESSION.* HIS BLOODIED HAND *TOUCHING* THE GROUND FOR BALANCE.

THAT WALL IS A GOOD TEN METERS HIGH.
NO *MAN* COULD POSSIBLY SCALE IT IN A SINGLE LEAP.

IF NO MAN COULD SCALE IT, WHAT DID?
YOU MEAN WHO DID?

IF YOU INTEND TO SOLVE THIS, YOU NEED TO KEEP AN OPEN MIND.
MY OPEN MIND TELLS ME THIS IS A JOB FOR THE POLICE.
THE POLICE WERE NOT VISITED BY THE GHOST OF A MAN THEY'VE NEVER MET.

PRESUMPTION BEING I'VE NEVER MET DICKENS.
BESIDES, GHOSTS DON'T EXIST.

IS THERE NO PART OF YOU THAT WISHES TO BELIEVE IN AN AFTERLIFE?

IF THE KILLER, MAN OR OTHERWISE, INSISTS ON PRESENTING HIMSELF A MONSTER, THEN WE SHOULD SPEAK WITH A MONSTER EXPERT OF OUR OWN.
DO YOU KNOW SOMEONE?

UNFORTUNATELY, I DO.

OWW!
HE BIT ME, AGAIN!
BRAM!

I RESPECT YOUR TALENT AND DEDICATION AS AN ACTOR--

--BUT REALLY, GEORGE--
I JUST WANT TO BREATHE LIFE INTO THIS DIABOLICAL MONSTER YOU'VE SO MASTERFULLY CREATED.
I UNDERSTAND, BUT IF YOU WERE AN ACTUAL VAMPIRE--

--I'D HAVE TO DRIVE THIS STAKE THROUGH YOUR CHEST, CUT OFF YOUR HEAD, AND BURN IT.

I SHOULD APOLOGIZE TO LUCY.
BRILLIANT.

THAT WAS A JOKE, YES?
HARD TO TELL WITH STOKER. HIS BELIEF IN THE SUPERNATURAL IS UNPARALLELED.
LET'S GET THE INFORMATION WE NEED AND BE ON OUR WAY.
DOYLE?

HERE HE COMES. IF HE MENTIONS THE "BIG BOOK", DO CHANGE THE SUBJECT.
WHAT'S THE BIG BOOK?

I CAN GET YOU OPENING NIGHT TICKETS, ARTHUR.
NO NEED TO SNEAK INTO DRESS REHEARSAL.

I'M HERE ON MORE SERIOUS MATTERS.
OF COURSE, WHY WOULD ANYONE TAKE DRACULA SERIOUSLY?

MR. HOUDINI.
YOU KNOW WHO I AM?
I HAVE AN EYE FOR TALENT. TELL ME, EVER ACCIDENTALLY SAWN SOMEBODY IN HALF?

NO.

BUT IF YOU WANTED TO--

--COULD YOU?

FORGIVE ME, I HAVE A GALLOWS SENSE OF HUMOR.

I'M CERTAIN YOU'RE **AWARE** OF THE GHASTLY MURDER LAST EVENING.
HOW WOULD YOU KNOW THAT?
YOU'RE HOLDING A COPY OF THE *PAPER.*
YES, WELL...

HARRY AND I WERE ***DISCUSSING*** THE DETAILS THIS MORNING--
--AND BELIEVED I'D BE THE MAN TO SHED ***LIGHT*** ON THE SUBJECT?

I DO HAVE MY THEORIES, BUT I HAVE YET TO CONSULT MY ***BIG BOOK.***
LATEST SPECIAL
FULL REPORTS
WOULD YOU LIKE TO SEE IT?

NO NEED FOR THAT--
WE ***CERTAINLY*** WOULD.

RIGHT THIS WAY THEN.

THUD

EVERYTHING YOU NEED TO KNOW ABOUT THE VARIOUS DARK FORCES THAT SURROUND US ARE IN THIS BOOK.
IT'S A CULMINATION OF MY *SCHOLARLY* WORK.
MARVELOUS.

NOT EVERYONE *APPRECIATES* IT.
BRAM, WE SIMPLY WANT TO KNOW HOW A MAN DRESSED AS SPRING HEELED JACK--

A *MAN?*
WHEN CAUGHT, SPRING HEELED JACK IS *ALWAYS* A MAN.
WHICH IS REASON TO BELIEVE SPRING HEELED JACK HAS NEVER BEEN *CAUGHT!*

HOWEVER, I WILL CONCEDE SPRING HEELED JACK IS BY ALL ACCOUNTS NOT AN *APPARITION* OR *POLTERGEIST.*
ARTHUR *ENCOUNTERED* ONE OF THOSE LAST NIGHT.
FULL BODY MANIFESTATIONS
WRAITH

OH *DID* HE?
YOU'RE NOT HERE ON A WHIM. YOU'RE SNIFFING AROUND.
TELL ME, WHO DID YOU SEE?
IT'S NOT IMPORTANT.
IT WAS CHARLES DICKENS.

HE WARNED ARTHUR THAT SPRING HEELED JACK HAD RETURNED.
THAT BLOOD WOULD RUN!

SOUNDS LIKE A HARBINGER OF DOOM.

THEN WE MUST BE OFF!
WE? YOU HAVE A PLAY TO DIRECT.
MY ASSISTANT IS MORE THAN ABLE TO KEEP THE TRAIN MOVING.

BRAM, I MUST INSIST HOUDINI AND I WORK ALONE.
I FEAR YOU AND I WOULD NOT SEE EYE TO EYE ON HOW TO PROCEED.
NONSENSE. I HAVE NO PROBLEM *ACQUIESCING* TO THE WILL OF THE GROUP.

SHALL WE PUT IT TO A VOTE?

A HACKSAW?
UNEARTHING A CORPSE CAN BE A TRICKY BUSINESS.
BEST TO BE PREPARED.

THE GROUNDS-KEEPER SEALED THE GATES.
WE MUST BE QUICK.

JUDGING BY MY RESEARCH, SPRING HEELED JACK CAN ONLY BE ONE OF THREE THINGS--
A VAMPIRE, A REVENANT--WHICH IS A REANIMATED CORPSE--OR A HUMAN POSESSED.
OR HE'S A PERSON MASQUERADING AS THE BOGEYMAN.

A BOGEYMAN IS A FICTITIOUS MONSTER CREATED BY PARENTS TO SCARE CHILDREN.
YOU REALLY DO NEED ME.

ASKING DR. FRANKENSTEIN TO JOIN THE TEAM WAS A MASTER STROKE.
OPEN MIND, REMEMBER?

YOUR OPEN MIND IS ABOUT TO DISTURB THE ETERNAL REST OF A WELL RESPECTED PRIEST.
HE WOULDN'T WANT THIS.
HE'S DEAD. I DOUBT HE'D WANT THAT EITHER.
HAHA HA!

THE BEST WAY TO FIND OUT HOW SOMEONE DIED IS TO INSPECT THE BODY.
YOU OF ALL PEOPLE SHOULD KNOW THAT, DOYLE.

DO YOU HEAR THAT?
WHAT?
DIGGING.

A WORD, SIR.

WHAT ARE
YOU DOING WITH
THIS BODY?

CRASH

AHHH!

GO!
I'LL CATCH
UP!

WE'LL NEVER CATCH HIM!
THIS WAY.

FOLLOW THAT WAGON!

DO YOU HAVE A FIVER?

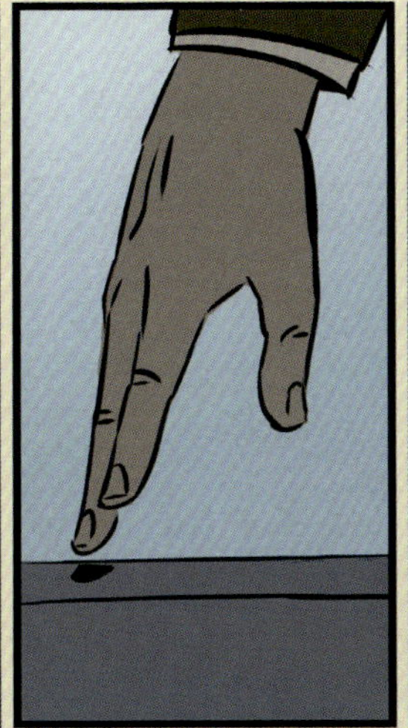

JUMP!

SIR, I DEMAND YOU--

WHAM
CRAAKKK
UP YOU GO!

THWWAACK

CRAASSHH

I WILL SUMMON YOU WHEN NEEDED.
UNTIL THEN, SCURRY BACK TO YOUR HOLE.

Chapter Three

KNOCK
KNOCK

KNOCK
BLOODY HELL.

MY APOLOGIES, INSPECTOR ATWOOD. WE WENT TO SCOTLAND YARD BUT THEY SAID YOU WERE *HOME*.
AS ONE WOULD EXPECT AT THIS *HOUR*. WHAT IN GOD'S NAME DO YOU WANT?
FATHER RAYNARD'S *BODY* HAS BEEN STOLEN.

HOW WOULD YOU KNOW THAT?

WE WERE AT HIS *GRAVE*, PAYING OUR RESPECTS.

SOMEONE IN LONDON --
OR SOME-THING --
THIS ALL MAKES SENSE NOW.

IF YOU WANT TO BE TAKEN SERIOUSLY, DON'T INVOLVE COUNT DRACULA.

CHECK THE GRAVE.
IT WAS A TRANSFER!
TRANSFER?
I'VE SEEN THE PAPERWORK MYSELF.
WAS THE PAPERWORK SIGNED, SPRING HEELED JACK?

WE WERE ATTACKED --
THIS IS MY INVESTIGATION. IF YOU ATTEMPT TO INVOLVE YOURSELF AGAIN, YOU'LL BE DOING SO DOWN AT SCOTLAND YARD.

SLAM!

DO YOU HEAR THAT?

WHAT IS IT?

THE SOUND OF YOU NOT TELLING ME WHAT'S GOING ON.

I WAS AT ROSEWOOD.
THE CEMETERY? WHATEVER FOR?
LOOKING FOR ANSWERS.
ANSWERS TO WHAT?

KOFF, KOFF, KOFF!

ARE YOU NOT AFRAID?

I FEEL STRONG. I PLAN TO CONTINUE THIS WAY.
IF NOT, I'LL ENJOY HAUNTING YOU TILL THE END OF YOUR DAYS.

I DON'T FIND THAT HUMOROUS.
MY FATE DOES NOT FRIGHTEN ME AS MUCH AS IT DOES YOU.
I LIKE TO THINK OUR LOVE IS *ETERNAL*.

DO YOU REALLY BELIEVE THERE'S MORE TO THIS LIFE AFTER IT'S GONE?

I DO. MY GREAT HOPE IS THAT EVENTUALLY YOU WILL TOO.

BUT UNTIL THEN, STOP POKING AROUND THAT GRAVEYARD OR TRISTAN WILL HAVE YOU ARRESTED.

WHAT ABOUT TRISTAN?
ROSEWOOD IS OWNED BY THE HEMSFORD ESTATE.

ARE WE ON TIME? IS IT DONE CORRECTLY?
YES, BUT--

BLAH, BLAH, BLAH -- THAT'S ALL.
BAD TIME?

SOONER WOULD HAVE BEEN BETTER.
I'M TESTING MY NEWLY ERECTED POWER PLANT USING LONDON'S TRAMS. IT'S A BIG PRESENTATION. HOPEFULLY YOU AND YOUR LOVELY WIFE WILL BE THERE.
ARE YOU A FAN OF CHOO-CHOO TRAINS?

WHEN I WAS A CHILD, YES.

THE T.H. LONDON ELECTRICAL CORPORATION... IS THAT YOU?
DIDN'T THINK I HAD IT IN ME, DID YOU?

I'VE ALWAYS BELIEVED IN YOUR ABILITY TO --
THROW A GOOD PARTY? MY FAMILY SHARES THE SAME SENTIMENT. THERE'S MORE TO ME THAN FRIVOLITY.
QUITE A LOT MORE.
T.H. LONDON ELECTRICAL CO.

WHAT BRINGS YOU TO MY HUMBLE ABODE, ARTHUR?
FATHER RAYNARD.

A DEAR FAMILY FRIEND. I INVITED HIM TO THE PARTY, BUT GOD FORBADE IT.
IRONIC HOW A NIGHT OF DEBAUCHERY MIGHT HAVE SAVED HIS LIFE.

ARE YOU AWARE HIS BODY WAS TRANSFERRED?
IMPOSSIBLE. ALL TRANSFERS AT ROSEWOOD REQUIRE MY PERSONAL SIGNATURE, AND NO SUCH REQUEST HAS CROSSED MY DESK.
WHERE WAS HE TAKEN?
I WAS HOPING YOU WOULD KNOW.

I'M SORRY, ARTHUR. MY SECURITY NORMALLY RUNS A VERY TIGHT SHIP.
IT DOES MAKE ME WONDER --

WONDER WHAT?

WAIT HERE.

CLINK!

TRISTAN?

BOO!!!!

BAM

HAHA HA!
SORRY, I COULDN'T RESIST.

SOLID PUNCH. BOX MUCH?

AMATEUR, IN MY YOUTH. I COULD HAVE KILLED YOU.
LUCKY FOR US YOU DIDN'T.
I WANTED YOU TO SEE SOMETHING.

I WAS ROBBED THE NIGHT OF THE PARTY.
A TALISMAN...I REMEMBER.

EGYPTIAN, AFRICAN, ASIAN...THIS WHOLE ROOM IS FULL OF SUPERSTITIOUS IDOLATRY BELIEVED TO CONJURE LIFE FROM THE DEAD.
ALL PURE NONSENSE THAT MY GREAT GRANDFATHER BELIEVED IN, BUT PRICELESS NONSENSE.
IF THEIR PURPOSE IS TO RESURRECT FROM THE DEAD, COULD THERE BE ANY CONNECTION BETWEEN THE DISAPPEARANCE OF THE TALISMAN AND THE BODY OF FATHER RAYNARD?

ANYTHING IS POSSIBLE.

I SUSPECT LOMAX LUMINARY. ALWAYS RAMBLING ABOUT THE AFTERLIFE --
-- AND WE'VE BOTH WITNESSED HIS PENCHANT FOR BARGING INTO PLACES UNINVITED.

LORD HEMSFORD, INSPECTOR ATWOOD TO SEE YOU.
ATWOOD?
I REQUESTED HE HELP FIND MY STOLEN TALISMAN.
I'D LOVE TWO GREAT DETECTIVE MINDS ON THE CASE.

I FEAR HE FINDS ME MOST DISAGREEABLE--
-- IT'S BEST I TAKE MY LEAVE.
THE DOOR TO THE LEFT, DOWN THE HALL.

GRRRRRR

WHAM!

JEZEBEL, HEEL!

ATWOOD GOT YOU, TOO?
NO, SHE CONVINCED HIM YOU WOULD STOP MEDDLING.
SHE?
SHE FOUND US. WE HAD NO IDEA YOU WERE IN HERE.
LET ME GUESS, YOUR MOTHER HAD A VISION?
THANKS TO YOUR BIZARRE ANTICS, A VISION WASN'T NECESSARY.
YOUNG LADY, PLEASE RELAY TO MR. DOYLE THAT WE WILL PROVIDE PERMANENT ACCOMMODATIONS FOR HIM IF NECESSARY.
INSPECTOR ATWOOD --
I HEARD HIM.

WHILE A PERSONAL EMBARRASSMENT, THE EVENTS OF THE DAY HAVE PROVEN FRUITFUL --
AHEM.
-- NOW, WHAT DO WE KNOW --
POLICE STATION

DID YOU NOT HEAR INSPECTOR ATWOOD? YOU SHOULD BE GETTING **HOME.**
BOOKS DO NOT WRITE THEMSELVES YOU KNOW.

-- FATHER RAYNARD WAS MURDERED UNDER MYSTERIOUS CIRCUMSTANCES.
A MAN WORKING IN CONJUNCTION WITH SPRING HEELED JACK STOLE HIS BODY FROM THE GRAVE.
BOTH MEN **EXTRAORDINARY** IN NATURE.
TRISTAN NEVER APPROVED THE TRANSFER OF RAYNARD'S BODY, WHICH SUGGESTS --
SOMEONE ELSE DID!

BUT WHO?
POSSIBLY THE SAME PERSON WHO STOLE AN ARTIFACT DURING TRISTAN'S PARTY.
ONE THAT ALLEGEDLY GIVES **LIFE** TO THE **DEAD.**
OH --

-- HOW THE PLOT THICKENS. IT'S JUST LIKE ONE OF YOUR STORIES! OR, ACTUALLY --

-- ONE OF YOUR STORIES.

WHY ARE YOU STILL HERE?

LOMAX LUMINARY?
THE POLICE BROUGHT YOU IN FOR QUESTIONING?
I CAME TO WARN THEM OF AN EVIL SPIRIT AMONG US

YOU CONFESSED?

LISTEN TO ME. I COMMUNICATE WITH THE DEAD. THEY SAY LONDON IS DOOMED.
BLOOD... WILL... FLOW!

BLOOD WILL FLOW. THE SAME WORDS DICKENS USED, DOYLE.

I'VE BEEN SEARCHING EVERYWHERE FOR THIS!

I THOUGHT I HAD LOST IT.
PERHAPS DICKENS CAN BE OF MORE ASSISTANCE. THE GIRL DOES CLAIM HER MOTHER CAN SPEAK WITH THE DEAD.

MEDIUMS ARE ONLY SLIGHTLY MORE TRUSTWORTHY THAN LOMAX.

IF WE INTEND TO SOLVE THIS, WE MUST KEEP OUR MINDS OPEN, HOUDINI.

I CALL UPON YOU TO SHOW YOURSELF.
DON'T BE SHY. WE WELCOME ALL.

I FEEL A *PRESENCE.* IT DESPERATELY WANTS TO COMMUNICATE WITH YOU, BUT SOMETHING HOLDS IT BACK.
CHANNEL THROUGH ME...CHANNEL THROUGH ME.

RUMBLE

I'VE LOST IT... IT'S GONE. IF YOU'LL EXCUSE ME.

WAS THAT HELPFUL?

HALF A DAY WASTED.
LESSON LEARNED.
FROM STOKER, I EXPECT IT. NOT FROM YOU, DOYLE.

BAM!

WHAT DID I TELL YOU, ARTHUR --

-- I SAID, FIND STEVENSON!
IT'S DICKENS.
ARE YOU SURE?
CERTAIN. HE SPOKE OF STEVENSON THE NIGHT I MET HIM.
THE GIFT DOESN'T LIE WITH THE MOTHER.

FIND STEVENSON.
HOW?
YOU'VE ALREADY FOUND HIM!
ARE YOU THREE HUNGRY? THE BREAD'S A BIT CHARRED, BUT IT'S EDIBLE!

NO. THANK YOU.

ARE YOU SURE?

QUITE. WE MUST BE GOING.

MOTHER'S READINGS ARE AFFORDABLE, BUT *NOT FREE.*

AGATHA, *STOP.* THEY DIDN'T GET WHAT THEY CAME HERE FOR.
NO MOTHER. I THINK THEY DID.

DO YOU HAVE A FIVER?

WHAT DICKENS SAID ABOUT STEVENSON --

-- WHY DIDN'T YOU TELL US SOONER?
I THOUGHT IT WILDLY ABSURD --
-- STEVENSON HAS BEEN DEAD FOR SIX YEARS.

MORE ABSURD THAN BEING VISITED BY THE GHOST OF CHARLES DICKENS?
IF THERE ARE ANY OTHER ABSURDITIES YOU'D LIKE TO SHARE, NOW WOULD BE THE TIME.

HE SAID, "ONLY THE *INSPECTORS.*"
INSPECTORS? INSPECTOR ATWOOD WAS A DEAD END.
I DON'T BELIEVE THAT'S WHAT HE MEANT.

BEDLUM ASYLUM!

CAN YOU GET US INSIDE?
BEDLAM
I CAN GET US INTO ANYTHING. BUT IF WE LAND IN TROUBLE, GETTING *OUT* WILL BE THE PROBLEM.

IF ANYONE WOULD LIKE TO BACK OUT, NOW WOULD BE THE TIME.

DONG!!!

LOONEY. MINUTES TO BED. GET INSIDE.

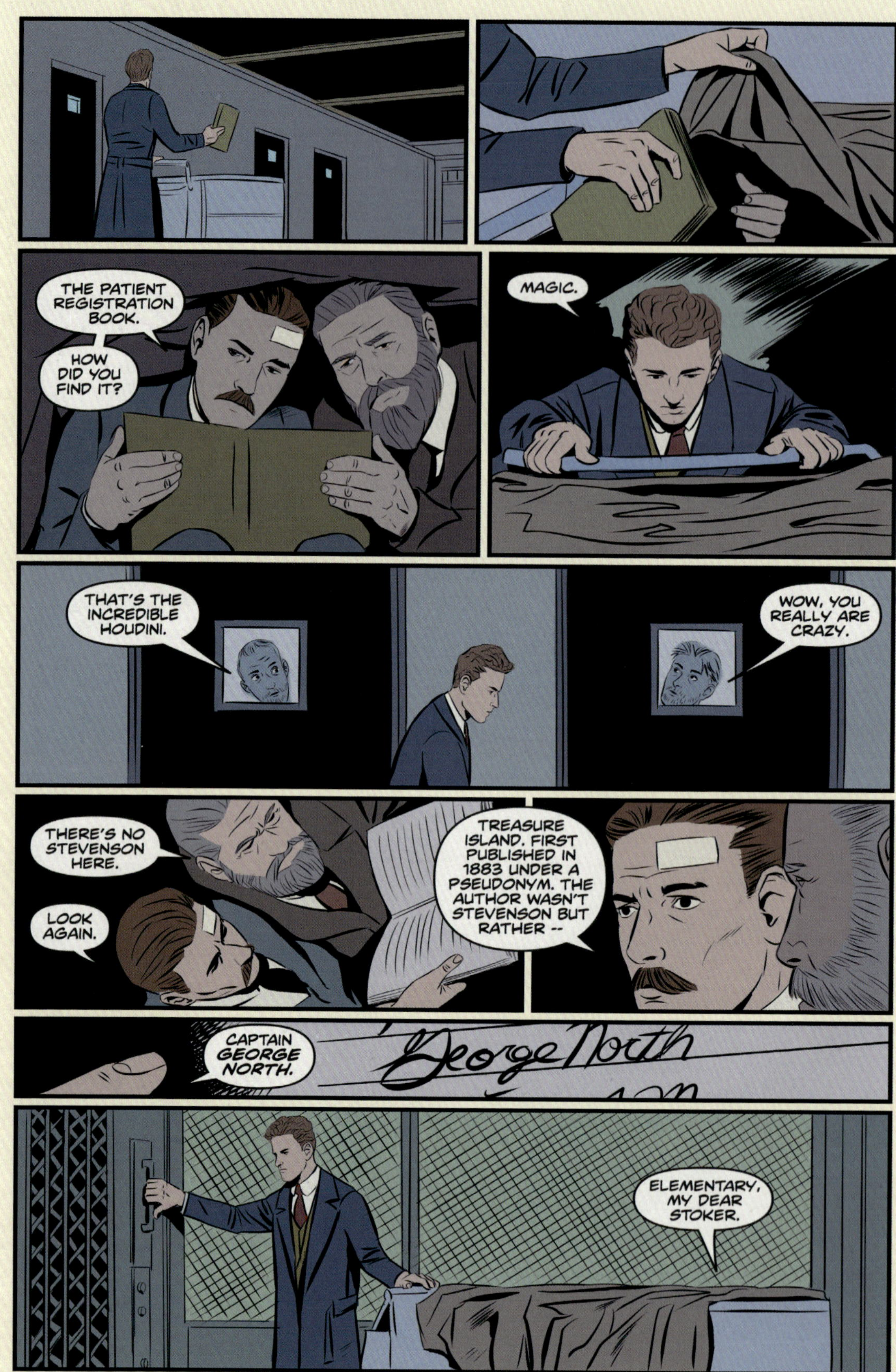

THE PATIENT REGISTRATION BOOK.
HOW DID YOU FIND IT?
MAGIC.
THAT'S THE INCREDIBLE HOUDINI.
WOW, YOU REALLY ARE CRAZY.
THERE'S NO STEVENSON HERE.
LOOK AGAIN.
TREASURE ISLAND. FIRST PUBLISHED IN 1883 UNDER A PSEUDONYM. THE AUTHOR WASN'T STEVENSON BUT RATHER --
CAPTAIN GEORGE NORTH.
George North
ELEMENTARY, MY DEAR STOKER.

ARGHHHHH!!!!
HELLO, HELLOOO, HEY!
A NAKED HOUSE, A NAKED MOOR, A SHIVERING POOL BEFORE THE DOOR.
DO YOU HEAR THAT?
A NAKED HOUSE, A NAKED MOOR, A SHIVERING POOL BEFORE THE DOOR.
I CANNOT HEAR ANYTHING WITH ALL THAT RACKET.
A GARDEN BARE --
-- OF FLOWERS AND FRUIT, AND POPLARS AT THE GARDEN FOOT.
I KNOW THIS POEM.
SUCH IS THE PLACE THAT I LIVE IN.

BLEAK WITHOUT AND BARE WITHIN.

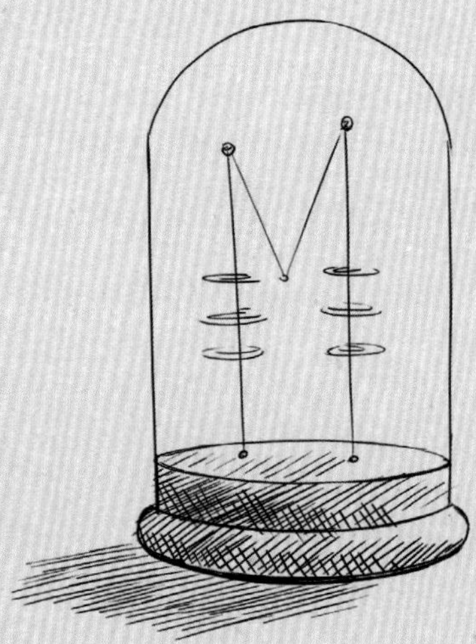

Chapter Four

THIS CANNOT BE THE GRAVEROBBER WE ENCOUNTERED.
IT IS.

DO I KNOW YOU?
PERHAPS.

WHAT IS YOUR NAME?
I CAN'T REMEMBER. THE NURSES CALL ME "GEORGE," BUT THAT'S NOT ME.
DOES "ROBERT" SEEM FAMILIAR?
NO.

HE'S MORE "HYDE" THAN STEVENSON.
I LIKE "HYDE."
WHY?

I DON'T KNOW.

COULD YOU LOOSEN HIS RESTRAINTS?
TRUST ME.

BLESSED ARE THE KIND.

WHAT HAVE YOU DONE WITH FATHER RAYNARD'S BODY?
WHO ARE YOU?
DO YOU KNOW WHO SPRING HEELED JACK IS?

TONIGHT... HE ARRIVES. TOMORROW IS THE END. YOU MUST LEAVE--
NOW!

OUR NEW FRIEND HAS BEEN COMING AND GOING AS HE CHOOSES. HE'S NO PRISONER; HE ONLY PRETENDS TO BE.
CLICK
HE IS HERE! HE WILL PUNISH US ALL!

KRAK

CRUNG

CLANG

KLONG

KRACK

POW

WHOMPF

WHOOSH

BOOOM

WHUMP

SLIIINNNG

SWOOM

WHAM

HE'LL BE FINE. IT'S DESIGNED TO EASE ITS HOLD AS THE CAPTIVE RELAXES.

WHO ARE YOU?
WE MET MANY YEARS AGO.

MY OLD INSIGNIA.

YOU GAVE THIS TO ME AS A BOY.

IT'S GOOD TO SEE YOU AGAIN, YOUNG DOYLE.

WHAAAAAAA!!

GET HIM LOADED.

QUICKLY!

WHAT IN GOD'S NAME IS SHE DOING HERE?
SHE SAID SHE WAS WITH YOU!

I'LL TAKE THE REINS IF YOU DON'T MIND, YOUNG LADY.

I DON'T, IF YOU CAN STEER US PAST...

THAT!

FLASH

PAAAAP

KRAAK

THROOSH

GRAB THE BALLOONER! NOW!

IS THIS IT?
NO... I DON'T REMEMBER WHAT THAT IS.

BA-BUUN

WHOOOMP

FLLUUMP

Factory Row

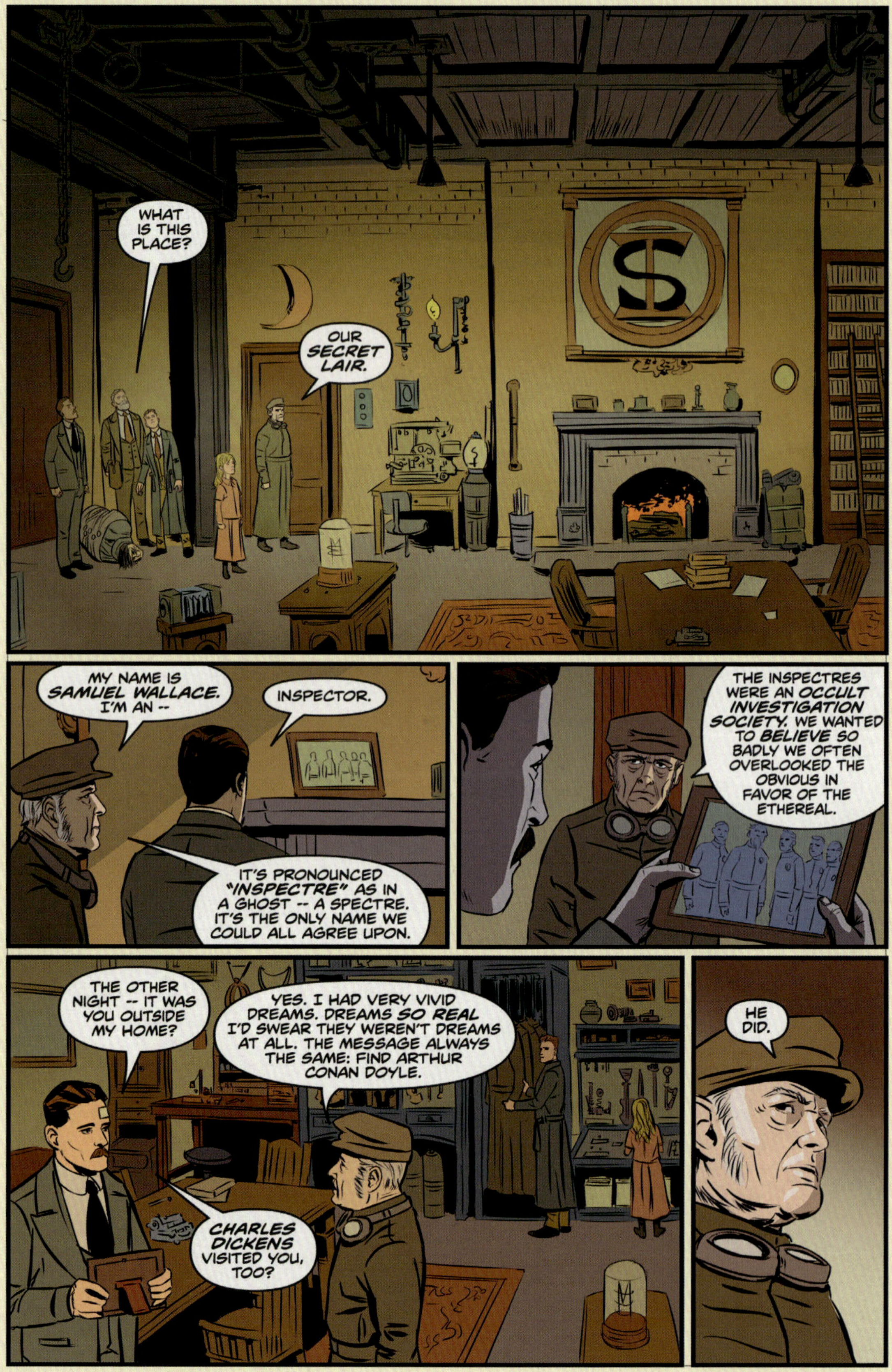

WHAT IS THIS PLACE?
OUR *SECRET LAIR.*

SCREEEEEECH

THAT IS NOT A *TOY!* PUT IT DOWN.

THE LOCAL IRONMONGER DOES NOT SELL GHOST CAPTURING TOOLS, SO WE MADE OUR OWN.
LIKE A SPIRIT, THESE DEVICES ARE A SHELL OF THEIR FORMER SELVES.
TREAD CAREFULLY WHEN NEAR.
FIFTH CENTURY SAXON --

-- WE'RE GOING TO NEED THESE.

WHAT'S THAT?
AN *INSPECTRAL BAROMETER.* IT'S USED TO DETECT AN INFLUX OF PARANORMAL ACTIVITY.

SO DICKENS ARRANGED ALL THIS FROM THE AFTERLIFE?
DICKENS SAID HE WOULD PROVE THE AFTERLIFE'S EXISTENCE --

-- FOR THE LONGEST TIME I REFUSED TO BELIEVE HIM.
AND NOW?
I'M AN OLD MAN... THE LAST INSPECTRE TO WALK ABOVE GROUND.

YOUR PRESENCE HAS PROVEN TO ME THAT DICKENS WAS CORRECT.
AND IF HE CONTINUES TO FIGHT IN THE NEXT LIFE, THEN SO MUST I IN THIS ONE.

Later
A TRANQUILIZER SHOULD KEEP HIM ASLEEP UNTIL WE KNOW HOW TO PROCEED.

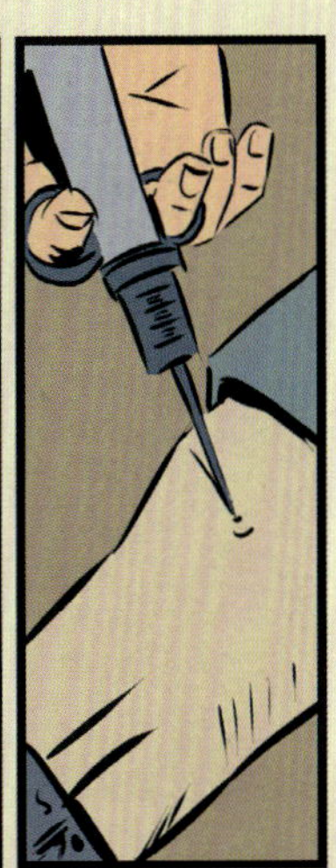

THOSE CHAINS WILL HOLD, YES?
YES.
CAN YOU SLIP OUT OF THEM?
I'M HARRY HOUDINI.

STOKER-- ANYTHING IN YOUR BIG BOOK ABOUT WHAT HE IS?

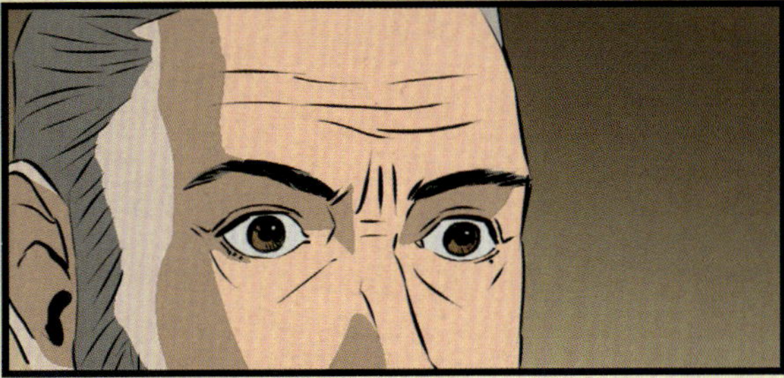

WALLACE, YOUR COPY OF ONE THOUSAND AND ONE NIGHTS, PLEASE.
OR AS IT'S TITLED IN THE MODERN ENGLISH: ARABIAN NIGHTS.
I DON'T KNOW IF I HAVE A COPY.
DICKENS SURELY WOULD HAVE.

THE ARABIAN NIGHTS
YOU'RE RIGHT.

ARABIAN MYTHOLOGY. THE FIRST KNOWN MENTION OF HYDE'S KIND. RIGHT HERE.
AFTER CAREFUL CONSIDERATION I CAN SAY WITH NEAR CERTAINTY...
... HYDE IS A GHOUL.

GHOULS ARE DEMONS: GRAVEYARD DWELLERS ASSOCIATED WITH THE CONSUMPTION OF HUMAN FLESH.
WE HAVE NO EVIDENCE OF THAT.
WOULD YOU LIKE TO VOLUNTEER YOUR HAND TO FIND OUT?

GHOULS ARE SHAPESHIFTERS, WHICH DESCRIBES THE GROSS MUSCULATURE.
SOME EVEN CLAIM THEY SERVE AS MINIONS TO VAMPIRES.
SOUND FAMILIAR?

YOU'RE IMPLYING THAT SPRING HEELED JACK IS A VAMPIRE?

OR A POSSIBLE VARIANT THEREOF.
HOW DOES THIS CONNECT TO STEVENSON?
CAN YOU NOT SEE IT, DOYLE? YOU SHOULD.
AFTER ALL, YOU DID CALL STEVENSON'S THE PAVILION ON THE LINKS THE "HIGH-WATER MARK OF GENIUS."

THE REVISED VERSION OF WHICH HE INCLUDED IN --
-- THE NEW ARABIAN NIGHTS.

THE MAN WHO WROTE THE STRANGE CASE OF DR. JEKYLL AND MR. HYDE WAS OBSESSED WITH THE GHOULS OF ANCIENT ARABIAN FOLKLORE.
HOWEVER, IT COULD JUST BE A COINCIDENCE.

WHAT DO WE DO WHEN HE WAKES UP?
ARTHUR, WHERE ARE YOU GOING?
TO GET SOME AIR. I NEED TO THINK.

RIIIINNNNGGGG

THE DOYLE RESIDENCE.
IT'S *ME*, DARLING.

OH, HELLO. HOW ARE *YOU*?
SOMETHING'S HAPPENED THAT I MUST TAKE CARE OF --

-- I'M AFRAID I WON'T BE HOME FOR A WHILE.
LOUISA?
I UNDERSTAND.
HOW ARE YOU FEELING?

GOOD.
BUT *HE'S NOT HERE* AT THE MOMENT.
THE *POLICE* ARE THERE?

YES.
I'M SORRY... I CAN EXPLAIN.
THAT WILL HAVE TO *WAIT*. WHEN HE RETURNS, I'LL TELL HIM YOU RANG.

CLICK

WHAT ARE YOU DOING HERE?
BRINGING YOU BACK. THE POLICE ARE SEARCHING FOR US.

YOU NEED TO GO HOME. YOUR FAMILY MUST BE WORRIED SICK.
I COULD SAY THE SAME FOR YOU.
PEOPLE ARE IN DANGER. IF MY PRESENCE CAN BE OF HELP, THEN I MUST STAY UNTIL OUR WORK IS DONE.

YOU MUST ADMIT I'VE BEEN USEFUL.
SURPRISINGLY.
I'M CURIOUS.

ABOUT?

IF THE INSPECTRES KNEW OF SPRING HEELED JACK, DO YOU THINK HE KNOWS OF THE INSPECTRES?

LET'S GO.

MASTER, I SAID NOTHING. I WAS LOYAL TO THE END.

I TOLD THEM NOTHING OF WHERE I TOOK THE BODIES! I SWEAR IT.

BODIES?

YES. THE...

... BODIES!

WHOUMPF!
CHING